BUG TEAM ALPHA
INVISIBLE
ENEMY

by Laurie S Sutton
illustrated by James Nathaniel

Raintree is an imprint of Capstone Global Library Limited, a
company incorporated in England and Wales having its registered
office at 264 Banbury Road, Oxford, OX2 7DY – Registered
company number: 6695582

www.raintree.co.uk
myorders@raintree.co.uk

Edited by Abby Colich
Designed by Kyle Grenz
Production by Katy LaVigne

ISBN 978-1-4747-4909-1 (paperback)
20 19 18 17
10 9 8 7 6 5 4 3 2 1

British Library Cataloguing in Publication Data
A full catalogue record for this book is available from
the British Library.

Acknowledgements
We would like to thank the following for permission to reproduce
photographs: Shutterstock: Mihai-Bogdan Lazar, throughout
(starfield), Somchai Som, throughout (Earth); Design elements:
Capstone and Shutterstock.

Every effort has been made to contact copyright holders of
material reproduced in this book. Any omissions will be rectified
in subsequent printings if notice is given to the publisher.

Printed and bound in China.

CONTENTS

MEET BUG TEAM ALPHA

Bug Team Alpha is the most elite Special Operations force of the Colonial Armed Forces of the Earth Colonial Coalition. Each member has an insect's DNA surgically grafted onto his or her human DNA. With special abilities and buglike features, these soldiers are trained to tackle the most dangerous and unique combat missions. Their home base is *Space Station Prime*.

Jackson "Vision" Boone

A human male with large eye grafts that resemble fly eyes. The eyes allow detection of multiple light spectra beyond human perception.

Rank: Commander
Age: 29 Earth Standard Years
Place of Origin: Planet Hephaestus
Hair: Light brown
Eyes: Fly eye graft
Height: 1.83 metres (6 feet)

Gustav "Burrow" Von Braun

A human male with digger beetle arms grafted onto his torso. He is heavyset and very strong and muscular.

Rank: Lieutenant
Age: 24 Earth Standard Years
Place of Origin: Earth,
        European Hemisphere
Hair: Brown
Eyes: Brown
Height: 1.68 metres (5 feet, 6 inches)

Anushka "Spoor" Kumar

A human female with combination DNA from several scenting insects. Nasal cavity folds open to expose scenting filaments that can detect even the smallest percentage of compounds in the air.

Rank: Lieutenant
Age: 28 Earth Standard Years
Place of Origin: Earth, Amaranth Colony
Hair: Brown
Eyes: Brown
Height: 1.65 metres (6 feet, 5 inches)

Irene "Impact" Mallory

A human female with a beetle exoskeleton grafted onto her body. She's always slightly hunched over like a linebacker ready to charge an opponent.

Rank: Lieutenant
Age: 24 Earth Standard Years
Place of Origin: Earth,
  European Hemisphere
Hair: Brown
Eyes: Brown
Height: 1.68 metres (5 feet, 6 inches)

Akiko "Radar" Murasaki

A human female with cranial antennae grafted onto her forehead. The antennae sense vibrations and can determine length between and shape of objects in dark spaces.

Rank: Lieutenant
Age: 28 Earth Standard Years
Place of Origin: Earth,
  Asian Hemisphere
Hair: Brown
Eyes: Brown
Height: 1.58 metres (5 feet, 2 inches)

Sancho "Locust" Castillo

A human male with wings and a dorsal exoskeleton grafted onto his body. He has immense strength and flying capabilities.

Rank: Lieutenant
Age: 23 Earth Standard Years
Place of Origin: Earth,
  South American Hemisphere
Hair: Light brown
Eyes: Brown
Height: 1.83 metres (6 feet)

CHAPTER 1

"Commander Boone, assemble a team and board the *Champion*, immediately," General Barrett ordered. Barrett was the highest-ranking officer in the Colonial Armed Forces. He was infamous for his brevity. "Planet Hephaestus is under attack. You'll be fully briefed on the ship."

"Yes, sir," replied Commander Jackson "Vision" Boone. He barely got the words out before the General's image vanished from the monitor just as quickly as it had appeared.

Although the details were sparse, Commander Vision knew exactly which Bug Team Alpha members would be suitable for a mission on Hephaestus. He loaded each member's information onto his wrist computer:

– – – – – – – – – –

Lt Akiko "Radar" Murasaki: Cranial Antennae DNA graft. Vibration detection. Age: 28 Earth Standard Years. Planet of origin: Earth, Asian Hemisphere.

– – – – – – – – – –

Lt Irene "Impact" Mallory: Beetle Exoskeleton DNA graft. High-impact tolerance and strength. Age: 24 Earth Standard Years. Planet of origin: Earth, European Hemisphere.

– – – – – – – – – –

Lt Gustav "Burrow" Von Braun: Digger Beetle arm and leg flange DNA graft. Enhanced tunnelling abilities and strength. Age: 24 Earth Standard Years. Planet of origin: Earth, European Hemisphere.

– – – – – – – – – –

Lt Sancho "Locust" Castillo: Locust DNA graft. Wings and dorsal exoskeleton. Heavy-duty flight and strength. Age: 23 Earth Standard Years. Planet of origin: Earth, South American Hemisphere.

– – – – – – – – – –

Lt Anushka "Spoor" Kumar: Experimental combination DNA graft from several scenting insects. A ridge on the nasal cavity folds opens to expose scenting filaments. Age: 28 Earth Standard Years. Planet of origin: Earth Colony Amaranth.

With his team's specs uploaded, Boone transmitted an order to each one of their wrist computers. The team members were to meet him aboard the *Champion* immediately.

✶ ✶ ✶

Seven Earth Standard Hours later, Commander Jackson "Vision" Boone led the five members of Bug Team Alpha into the briefing room aboard the troop transport ship, *Champion*. All any of them knew was that a distress call had come in from a colony within the Earth Colonial Coalition and that troops from the Colonial Armed Forces had been deployed.

The Bug Team was an elite, Special Operations team within the Colonial Armed Forces. Not only were they trained for unique and unusual missions, their bodies were specially designed for it. Genetic doctors had surgically grafted a different insect's DNA onto the human DNA of each member. This gave the members special powers. It also gave each one of them a specific insectlike appearance and abilities.

The team operated outside the normal chain of command. They reported only to General Barrett. This gave them the authority to act independently. It also allowed them access to the mission briefing aboard the *Champion*, which was usually reserved for command-rank officers.

The briefing room was compact. A large video monitor took up one wall. In front of the monitor was a podium. The room was empty when the team arrived. The task force commanders attending the briefing weren't there yet.

Even though there were chairs, Bug Team Alpha did not sit in them. Impact and Locust had external insectoid carapaces that were too bulky. They stood to one side of the room. The rest of the team stood with them.

"Any idea what this op is about?" Lt Sancho "Locust" Castillo whispered to Impact.

"Nope," Lt Irene "Impact" Mallory replied with a shrug of her large shoulders. Then she grinned at her winged teammate. "But we never get called up for the boring stuff."

Five task force commanders entered the briefing room. After everyone was settled, Mission Commander Cussler entered the room. The short and stocky man, about 40 Earth Standard Years, speedily walked up to the podium.

"A distress call has been received from the Colonial Governor of the mining planet, Hephaestus. The capital city of Talos has been attacked. We don't know anything about the attacker. All we have is this video," Cussler stated. Then he activated the briefing room's video monitor by pushing a tiny button on his wrist computer.

A video report began playing on the briefing room monitor. The rough and unsteady images came from the helmet cam of someone running down a street while dodging blaster fire.

A digital readout on the video identified the person as Lt Michelle Barr, a member of the Talos Police Force, along with date and time information.

The audio recorded the shouts and confusion of the other officers around her, also under fire.

"Watch out! It's coming from the left now!" someone warned as blaster fire streaked close by.

The side of a building exploded and threw debris at the camera. The image faltered and spun as Lt Barr dropped and rolled. Blaster fire filled the screen as she shot at an unseen enemy.

"Follow the blaster fire. Shoot at where it's coming from!" Barr shouted.

"How can you fight something you can't see!" a voice said angrily.

The helmet cam shifted as Lt Barr searched left and right trying to spot who was firing on her and the other officers. All her camera picked up was blaster fire coming at her but not who – or what – was firing it.

"Just fire in a wide sweep and hope you hit something!" Barr ordered.

The video report continued to display the lopsided firefight until Mission Commander Cussler discontinued the playback with a touch on his wrist computer.

"As the video shows, the people of Talos have come under attack, but no one has actually seen the enemy," Cussler stated. "It could be a cloaking tech or some other form of camo. We just don't know. Our mission is to defend the capital city of Talos and protect its population. Dropships deploy for the planet in 15 Earth Standard Minutes. Task force commanders, ready your troops. Dismissed."

As the commanders left the briefing room, Mission Commander Cussler took Vision aside.

"Commander Vision, I didn't know who General Barrett would assign to this mission. Now I see that your unique eyesight is perfectly suited to combat this 'invisible enemy'," Cussler said as he gestured at the commander's DNA-enhanced, insectlike eyes. "I'm glad to have you and Bug Team Alpha with us on this mission."

"Yes, sir," Vision replied and snapped a salute. Behind him the Bug Team saluted as a single unit.

"Dismissed," Cussler said as he marched from the briefing room.

"The mission is on planet Hephaestus?" Impact said as the Bug Team walked out of the room.

"Hey, Commander Vision, didn't you grow up on Hephaestus?"

Vision's shoulders got tense and he kept his gaze on the deck.

"Yes," was his only answer.

Vision stomped down the corridor as the rest of Bug Team Alpha followed.

"He's been prickly ever since he assembled this mission team," Lt Burrow observed as he scratched his head with one of his buglike arms.

"That's not like him. I wonder what's going on," Lt Impact said.

"Wait. Now I get it. You said it yourself, Impact – the commander is from Hephaestus. And now Hephaestus has been attacked," Lt Radar suddenly realized. "No wonder he's been upset."

"Do you think he still has family there?" Lt Spoor asked.

"He's doesn't talk much about his past," Burrow mentioned.

The commander didn't hear his teammates. He was so distracted by thoughts of his home planet, he didn't see a group of approaching Coalition troopers until he almost ran into them.

"What are you – ! Slow down grunt!" one of the troopers snapped. He shoved Vision without thinking.

All other members of Bug Team Alpha surged forwards, getting in the trooper's face. But the trooper's pals lined up beside their comrade.

"Oh. I get it. You're those altered guys," the trooper sneered.

"You mean enhanced," Impact replied and stepped even closer.

"You're big, bug, but you don't scare me," the trooper replied. "Your kind is . . ."

"Trooper! Name and rank!" came a sharp, commanding voice.

"Uh, uh, Private Margate! Sir!" the soldier responded immediately and snapped to attention.

He looked around for who had barked the order. It took him a few seconds to realize that the voice had come from one of the "altered guys" standing in front of him. Commander Vision tapped his rank insignia.

"Dismissed!" Vision said sharply.

The troopers obeyed, but they muttered as they left. Radar's genetically engineered cranial antennae quivered as she received the vibrations of their parting comments: "Freaks."

Lt Radar didn't tell her teammates what she had heard. Many people didn't approve of the genetic engineering that had created Bug Team Alpha. While dozens of humanoid species made up the Earth Colonial Coalition, the half-insect, half-human Bug Team was still looked upon as abnormal.

Suddenly, a loud, ship-wide alert sounded.

BUZZZZZ. BUZZZZZ.

It was time to load the troops onto the dropships.

Bug Team Alpha was only a small part of the total force heading for the capital city of Talos. Mission Commander Cussler was in charge of 1,000 soldiers. The troops were divided into five companies of 200 soldiers. Each company was led by its own task force commander.

Commander Vision led his team onto their assigned dropship. They climbed into combat armour mounted on harnesses on the ship's bulkhead.

Locust and Impact didn't need artificial armour. Their hard, beetle DNA-enhanced carapaces were their protection. They strapped on their weapons and emergency medical packs and grabbed their helmets.

"Look who we're sharing a ride with," Burrow said as he nodded to Private Margate and his buddies suiting up down the line.

"Ignore them and concentrate on our mission," Vision ordered. "Strap in. Hephaestus has a rough atmosphere."

A moment later they felt the dropship shudder as it detached from the *Champion*. It wasn't long before everyone bounced in their harnesses as the dropship bumped through the rough atmosphere.

Vision listened to the command chatter over the miniature speaker attached to his ear. There were five dropships, and they were each ordered to land in separate sections of the city. Vision felt their vessel bank sharply and then fire its vertical landing engines. The ship touched down. Immediately, the main troop deployment hatch opened. The troop harnesses released automatically.

Bug Team Alpha had been the last ones to board the dropship, which positioned them to be the first ones out. Commander Vision led his team down the hatch ramp in full combat mode.

"Mission orders are to protect and defend the citizens of Talos!" Vision told the team over the comm. "The enemy is basically invisible. Be on the highest alert!"

Bug Team Alpha did not know what they'd find once they stepped off the dropship. They had braced themselves for anything. They were still staggered by what they saw.

CHAPTER 2

Talos was a skeleton of its former self. Buildings were reduced to rubble. Columns of smoke rose into the air from unseen fires. Vision led Bug Team Alpha straight into the ruins. Behind them, Task Force Commander Kurosawa led his company of troops from the dropship and into the wreckage.

"Be on the alert. The enemy could still be here," Vision warned. "Locust, go aloft for recon. Impact, Burrow, take point. Radar, Spoor, scan for vibrations and scents."

As his team deployed using their special skills, Vision searched the surrounding area with his bug-enhanced sight. He could see beyond the normal human spectrum with his DNA-enhanced compound eyes.

Commander Vision was shocked to see that the city he had grown up in was now a smoking ruin. Thousands of people lived in Talos. Many of them were miners that worked in the huge Talos Mine.

Hephaestus was famous for its industrial ores and precious metals. The Talos Mine produced valuable Talo-Titanium used in the construction of spaceship hulls. It's how the capital city got its name and why it attracted people and businesses that supported the mining industry. But it was also a vibrant metropolis with restaurants, art and entertainment. Now, Vision didn't recognize the place.

Kurosawa fanned his troops out behind the Bug Team. The area was eerily silent. The only sound came from the Coalition forces walking over large piles of loose stone and masonry, which was all that was left of the buildings. They made their way for about 100 metres without encountering any resistance or attack. If the enemy was still here, it was not engaging. Or maybe it was just waiting.

"Something's coming up from below!" Radar shouted suddenly. She aimed her blaster as her cranial antennae pointed at a heap of rocks near her feet.

Private Margate and his buddies were closest to her position and converged on the spot. They surrounded Radar with their fingers on their triggers, ready to shoot.

"Hold your fire!" Commander Vision shouted as he ran to Radar's side. He stared down at the tumble of rocks. "I see a heat signature under there! It's human!"

Burrow ran over. He dug through the rubble with his sturdy arm spikes. Impact used her strength to help hurl away large chunks of debris as if they were only pebbles. A few moments later, the frightened face of a young boy looked up at the unusual features of the Bug Team members. He suddenly looked even more afraid.

"Don't worry. We're here to help," Radar said as she smiled and held out her hand. Vision had been right, the child was human, and he looked to be about 10 Earth Standard Years old. "Bug Team Alpha, at your service. My call sign is Radar, but my real name is Akiko. What's yours?"

"Darrin," the boy replied as he took Radar's hand.

"Hi, Darrin. You're safe now," Radar assured him as she lifted him out of a pocket in the rubble.

"My family is still down there," Darrin said shakily.

"We'll find them," Radar promised. She poked her head down into the hole and scanned with her antennae. "I feel voices coming from three metres south of our position, " she told Burrow.

Burrow started to dig. Soon more survivors crawled out of the ruins. Darrin ran over and hugged one of them – his mum.

"It looks like our mission has gone from defend and protect to search and rescue," Commander Kurosawa told Commander Vision.

"Looks that way," Vision replied. "I've got to get to the city's assembly hall. I have to find the governor of Talos."

"My troops can handle things here," Kurosawa said.

Bug Team Alpha followed as Vision ran across the jumbled ruins. He sprinted in one direction, paused, and then headed in another direction. At last he stopped and turned around in a circle.

"I can't find it. I don't recognize a single thing. Everything I knew is gone," Vision said. "I don't even know what street we're on."

"What are we looking for, sir?" Spoor asked.

"The city's assembly hall in the centre of Talos," Vision replied. There was an edge of worry in his voice. "But I can't find it. All the landmarks have been destroyed."

"I can get a better perspective from up here, sir," Locust declared as he buzzed above them. He flew so high that the team could not see him, but his voice soon came over the comm system loudly and clearly. "Found it!"

Locust transmitted the coordinates to the team's wrist computers. They scrambled over mounds of stone and polycrete rubble to reach his location. They found Lt Locust standing atop the ruins of a collapsed building. The team started to dig immediately. Burrow used his DNA-enhanced digger arms. Impact used her strength. The other Bug Team members used their hands.

"I am going to recommend that going forward shovels should be a standard part of our combat gear," Radar mentioned breathlessly.

"I smell people!" Spoor shouted as she cleared a small opening.

"I feel voices!" Radar confirmed.

The team widened the gap and Vision peered inside.

"I can see multiple heat signatures," the commander announced. "Let's make a bigger hole!"

Lt Burrow cleared a wide vertical shaft down through the rubble of the collapsed building. Bug Team Alpha dropped down on ropes into what was left of the assembly hall. The room was dark and the air was full of dust.

"Helmets on! Lights on!" Vision ordered.

Their lights revealed a group of 15 men and women huddled against a wall in what used to be the main meeting chamber.

"Thank goodness you found us!" one of the men declared. Vision recognized him.

"Councillor Vargas, are you all right?" Vision asked.

"Yes, but it was close! The Council was in session when the building collapsed," Vargas said.

The team immediately provided first aid from the medical supplies in their emergency medical packs. Fortunately, they only had to treat some minor cuts and bruises.

Commander Vision looked around the darkened room with his enhanced sight as if searching for a specific person.

"If the Council was in session, then the governor was here. Where is he?" Vision asked. His voice was full of concern.

"Here I am! What's going on in here?" the governor replied irritably as he limped in from another chamber.

"Dad!" Commander Vision exclaimed and rushed forwards to hug the governor.

"Dad?" the rest of the Bug Team echoed.

The colonial governor halted in his tracks when he saw Commander Vision – his genetically altered son. His already irritated expression deepened and turned cold. Vision faltered in his steps towards his father and then came to a stop. No hugs were exchanged.

"It's about time the Coalition forces got here!" the governor complained. "For all the good it did to save Talos."

Vision did not respond. Even though 1,000 troops scrambled to reach Talos in less than eight Earth Standard Hours, he knew it would not satisfy his father. Nothing did.

"Are you injured? Do you require medical attention?" Vision asked, falling back on protocol.

"No. Just get me out of here. I need to talk to your commanding officer," the governor growled.

Even though Vision was the commanding officer on site, he did not correct his father. Vision contacted Mission Commander Cussler and reported the current status of the colonial governor.

"Bring him to my command base," Cussler said. "I've constructed a temporary field office. Transmitting the coordinates now."

"Yes, sir," Vision replied. His wrist computer downloaded the data. Then he transferred the information to Lt Locust. "Take the governor to Mission Headquarters, please."

"Yes, sir!" Locust said. He wrapped his arms around the governor and buzzed up through the hole the Bug Team had created.

"No! Not one of you fr–," the governor protested, but it was too late. Locust carried the startled man up through the vertical shaft and out of sight.

CHAPTER 3

As the rest of Bug Team Alpha tended to the wounded council members, Commander Vision went through the other rooms in the building searching for survivors. There was no light, but Vision didn't need it. His compound eye structure let him see in the infrared spectrum. It was like having built-in night vision goggles.

Vision turned off his helmet light, which made it easier for him to scan the collapsed halls and chambers for red-spectrum body heat. The commander was surprised when he saw a large, vaguely humanoid shape in the ultraviolet range. Even with his insect DNA-enhanced eyesight, the image wasn't completely clear to him.

Vision slowly took a few steps forwards. Suddenly, the image moved. Fast. It retreated further down the half-collapsed corridor. The commander drew his weapon and followed.

"Vision to Bug Team. I'm in pursuit of . . . I don't know what it is," Vision reported over the comm to his team.

"We're on our way," Radar responded.

"No, I can follow for now. Everyone, stay back for medical aid," Vision replied. "Besides, this might be nothing."

"Standing by," Radar confirmed.

The commander worked his way through a dark maze of crushed masonry. The whole area was severely unstable. Dust rained down on him at the slightest movement.

"I can't seem to catch another glimpse of whatever this thing is," Vision reported. "But I can hear it moving ahead of me. It isn't being subtle. I'm following the sound."

Vision crawled over the top of a pile of rubble just in time to see the debris in front of him slide as if something invisible was climbing over it. Suddenly, a hole opened up in the ceiling, leading to the street above.

"It's heading topside!" Vision shouted over the comm as he bolted as fast as he could towards the opening.

The commander climbed up the mound of debris and out of the hole. When he got onto the street level, the surrounding area was quiet and still. Rubble was everywhere. He spun a full 360 degrees but could not detect anything moving in any spectrum.

"Whatever it was, it's gone," Commander Vision reported. "Heading back to your location."

Vision rejoined his team. Commander Kurosawa had arrived with several squads of soldiers. They were there to help rescue the government officials and any other people trapped in the assembly building. Civilian volunteers were also pitching in.

The people of Talos were starting to come out of their hiding places now that the Coalition Armed Forces had arrived. Locust returned to the site as Commander Vision gathered the Bug Team for their next move.

"I spotted a humanoid form down in the corridors that registered in the ultraviolet spectrum," Vision told his team. "If it's one of our invisible enemies, I have an idea how to detect them. Mount the UV scopes on your blasters. We're going on a hunting expedition."

The day was turning to night as the commander led his team to the area where he lost track of the strange humanlike form. The Bug Team looked through their UV scopes as they searched in a grid pattern, using the escape hole as the centre point.

Radar scanned for unusual vibrations with her antennae. Spoor opened her nasal flaps as wide as possible and "sniffed" for unfamiliar scents. Locust flew recon above his teammates. They couldn't use their night vision goggles while scanning with the UV scopes.

Everyone except Commander Vision was limited in their visual range, but that did not slow down Bug Team Alpha. The team did not know exactly what they were looking for, but they were ready for anything they found.

"Got movement," Radar warned quietly over the comm.

The rest of the team pivoted to face in her direction.

"Never mind. It's just rats," she said.

"Phew! They stink!" Spoor commented and almost sneezed.

The clear sound of breaking glass alerted the team to something in a nearby building. Bug Team Alpha turned in that direction in unison.

"Nothing in the UV spectrum," Vision whispered over the comm.

"Limited movement. Large vibration outline. It's big," Radar reported.

"And it stinks worse than the rats," Spoor added.

"Move in," the commander ordered.

The Bug Team worked their way over the rubble as quietly as possible. They moved in and surrounded the unknown enemy with blasters raised.

"Identify yourself!" Commander Vision declared.

"Uh, uh, Rontis Fontis," the human voice replied. "Um . . . I work here?"

Burrow spun the person around to face the Bug Team. The man's bulky coat flapped open. Inside was stolen jewellery and other valuables hanging out of multiple inner pockets.

"Pheeeew!" Spoor gasped at the odour of his furry garment. "That's what I smelled."

"He's a looter," Impact growled.

"I'm self-employed," the man corrected.

"Whatever. We don't have time for this," Commander Vision said. "Locust, escort this thief to a security station."

"Yes, sir!" Locust replied. He held his breath, wrapped his arms around him, and flew off with the man.

Bug Team Alpha resumed their search pattern. They tensed every time they heard sounds of movement in the fallen rubble. Every time it turned out to be rats.

"I hate rats," Impact grumbled.

"I hate spiders," Radar sympathized.

Another heap of debris shifted in front of the team members. They aimed their UV scopes, expecting to see more rats. Instead, several large humanoid shapes loomed in UV scope lights. The shapes fired on Bug Team Alpha.

Blaster fire lit the dark ruins like lightning. Commander Vision tried to spot the ultraviolet enemy, but the bright blaze of the firefight confused his sight.

"Fire in a wide sweep! Shoot at wherever their blaster fire is coming from!" Vision ordered. "Now I know what the police officer in the video report was going through."

"I've got 'em in my UV scope!" Impact declared just before she charged across the rubble at full speed.

The ultraviolet beam of Impact's UV scope revealed three humanoid shapes just before she rammed into them. Her headlong rush carried her into the side of a ruined building. The impact stunned her and she fell. The enemy blaster fire stopped.

"You got 'em!" Vision said.

The Bug Team rushed over to their dazed comrade, but there was no visible sign of the enemy when they got there.

"They got away!" Burrow growled.

"Not completely. One of them left a trail," Vision said.

The commander pointed at a glowing, crystalline liquid spattered on the nearby rubble. It sparkled in the dark as he dragged his gloved fingers though it. The liquid stuck to the glove. The beams from the UV scopes made it light up.

"It looks like we wounded one of them," Commander Vision concluded. He called Mission Commander Cussler on the comm immediately.

"Sir, I have new intel on the invisible enemy," he reported.

CHAPTER 4

As late night turned to early morning, the sun rose over Talos. Commander Vision, the task force commanders and Colonial Governor Jefferson Boone, met with Mission Commander Cussler. They gathered in a compact polycrete-and-steel structure soldiers had built near one of the dropships. It served as Cussler's temporary Mission Headquarters.

"There has been a change in orders," Commander Cussler announced. "We are to immediately begin evacuating Talos. Additional Coalition forces are being sent as reinforcements to fight this invisible enemy. Civilians can't be risked in the battle."

"Absolutely not!" Governor Boone exclaimed. "I'm not leaving, and neither are any of the miners. We don't abandon our mines."

Governor Boone glared pointedly at Commander Vision as he made that last remark. The other commanders took notice, especially Cussler.

"It's true," Vision replied much to the surprise of the governor. "Miners do not abandon their mines. It's a long-standing tradition of our . . . I mean . . . of the mining profession."

"I respect that, Commander, Governor Boone. But I have my orders from General Barrett himself," Cussler said. "The people of Talos will be evacuated. It's a matter of safety."

The governor stomped out of the meeting, frustrated. Cussler dismissed his commanders. As the officers left, Cussler asked Vision to stay.

"You reported last night that the Bug Team engaged the enemy and discovered that they can be detected using ultraviolet light," Cussler said. "Excellent work. I've ordered all troops to use UV scopes. And I'm awarding you a combat commendation."

"Yes, sir. Thank you, sir," Vision replied crisply.

"Is it hard for you to accept praise, Commander Vision?" Cussler asked.

"I . . . I don't understand, sir," Vision stumbled. He did not expect this question from his superior officer.

"I know officers that wear their medals on their pyjamas. And all I get from you is 'Yes, sir, thank you, sir',” Cussler said as he turned his attention to his wrist computer.

Commander Vision waited to be dismissed. And waited. Cussler seemed to be taking a very long time on the computer.

“Ah. Now I understand the dynamic,” Cussler said at last as he looked up from a bio displayed on his wrist computer. “Governor Boone is your father. You were born here, but left. You're a miner who abandoned his mine.”

“It's no secret, sir,” Vision replied.

“The tension between you two in the meeting was obvious,” Cussler observed.

“It won't interfere with the mission's success, sir,” Vision stated.

“No, it won't. At least not on your part,” the mission commander said.

Vision wasn't sure if that was meant as a compliment or a warning.

“You are now dismissed,” Cussler finished.

Vision left and walked out onto the ruined streets of Talos, his hometown. But he was not taking a nostalgic stroll. He was looking for the metallurgy labs on Ore

Street, where miners took new, unidentified samples to be analysed.

The streets were wrecked. Not much was recognizable, but Vision finally found his way. He was glad to see that at least one lab had survived the destruction. He smiled when he saw the name above the door: Jake's. Vision remembered coming here as a kid with his mineral "treasures." That is, before he became Vision.

He went inside. Nothing had changed. He rang the old-fashioned bell on the service counter.

"I can't help you! I'm evacuating!" a voice shouted from a back room.

Vision walked around the service counter and into the back. The voice belonged to an old man. He was packing up equipment. Vision recognized the balding, older man.

"Jake," Vision said. "It's good to see you again."

"Wait. I know that voice. Jack? Jackson Boone?" Jake laughed and turned around to face Vision.

The old man's face changed from pleasant surprise to startled discomfort. He stared at the large compound bug eyes.

"Yeah, Jake, it's me. I've had a little work done," Vision tried to reassure the man. "Heck of a time for a homecoming, huh?"

"Uh, yeah. It's good to see you . . . ," Jake stumbled over his words and looked away from Vision's eyes.

"Don't worry, I'm used to it," Vision said. "After the mining accident, everything got fixed up except my eyes. I was blind. But the doctors told me about the Interspecies Genetics Programme that was part of the Special Operations division. I got my sight back, and then some."

"Your father never said anything about why you didn't come back home," Jake said.

"Dad didn't approve of the surgery," Vision replied.

"Your father is a hard man to please," Jake observed.

"Jake, I need you to analyse something for me," Vision said, changing the conversation. He handed Jake a combat glove streaked with dried crystalline liquid. The substance caught Jake's attention immediately.

"What is it?" Jake asked as he put on a pair of magnifying goggles.

"You tell me. That's why I'm here," Vision replied.

Jake forgot about his packing and put the glove under a large spectrometer to test its optic properties. He frowned at the readouts. He scraped a sample from the glove and took it to a machine that would test its density and hardness. Again, he frowned at the results. At last Jake put the sample under a powerful microscope to study the crystalline structure.

"What is th–!" Jake exclaimed. "This isn't like anything I've ever seen before. It has an organic component. It's similar to blood. What's this from?"

"It's from the enemy that's been attacking Talos," Vision replied. "If that liquid is blood, then all my theories go out the airlock. I thought the enemy might be robotic or synthetic constructs. This means they're alive."

"I've done all that a metallurgist can do to analyse the stuff," Jake said. "You might want to consult someone trained in organic examination."

"You mean a doctor?" Vision asked.

"Yep," Jake replied and went back to packing.

CHAPTER 5

Commander Vision made his way to a temporary field hospital that had been constructed near one of the dropships.

Inside the structure was the field office of Dr Perinoff, the chief medical officer for the mission. Vision walked past rows of beds where medical personnel were caring for the wounded. He ignored all the startled looks.

"Dr Perinoff, do you have a moment?" Vision asked as he stood in the open doorway of the man's office.

"Sure. What can I-?" The physician stopped in mid sentence as he looked up from his paperwork and saw Commander Vision.

The commander braced himself for yet another shocked reaction, but was surprised when the doctor jumped up from his chair with a wide smile. He even held out his hand in greeting.

"Come in! Come in!" Perinoff invited the commander. "I'm so pleased to meet you. Commander Vision, right? I've heard all about Bug Team Alpha!"

The tall, thin doctor with dark skin and hair shook Vision's hand enthusiastically.

"I've studied the surgical procedures of the Interspecies Genetics Programme," Perinoff said. "Fascinating work! Gene splicing and recombination at the highest level. Enhancing DNA. Incredible. I'm a real fan!"

"Um, thanks?" Vision replied.

"Your eye graft was developed from the enhanced DNA of an ordinary household fly, correct?" Perinoff asked.

He leaned in to peer at Vision's compound orbs.

"Not that you are ordinary, commander! Not ordinary in the least!" he observed.

"No. Um, doctor, I need your help," Vision said.

"Oh! Of course. Are you ill? Are you in pain?" the physician asked. "Your grafts can tolerate standard medications I believe. I don't recall reading about any side effects or complications."

"Not that kind of help," Vision replied. He showed Perinoff the combat glove with the dried crystalline liquid on it. "I need you to analyse this."

"What is it?" the doctor asked as he took the glove from the commander.

"I'm not sure. I need a second opinion," Vision said.

"Another doctor has seen this already?" Perinoff asked. He sounded a little annoyed.

"No. I showed it to a metallurgist first," Vision told the doctor. "It appears to be crystal but with organic components."

"Organic? How . . . ? Never mind. Let's find out," the physician said.

Perinoff led Vision to a small lab. He examined the material on the glove with a microscope. He frowned at the results. Then the doctor dropped a sample into a magnetic compound separator to break down the substance into its basic elements. The readings made him frown some more.

"That's the same expression Jake, my friend the metallurgist, had," Vision observed.

"It's almost like blood," Perinoff said.

"That's the same thing Jake said," the commander replied.

"Really. You're comparing me to a rock chemist," the doctor grumbled. "Hmmm. One more test will give us the answer to this crystal riddle."

Perinoff put a sample onto a metal plate and slid it into what looked like a horizontal toaster.

"It's an electro conductivity monitor," the doctor explained. "This will show us if the sample can carry an electrical charge."

A graph on the monitor spiked immediately.

"Yes! This stuff isn't exactly blood. It's more like a super-conductive medium," the doctor concluded.

"Um, explain that in terms a Bug like me can understand," Vision requested.

"It's like the fluid in our nerves and spinal column that carry nerve impulses," Perinoff replied. "Without it we're paralyzed."

"Paralyzed? That means if we can find a way to disrupt this fluid we might have just found the way to defeat our invisible enemy!" Vision said and shook the physician's hand.

The commander left the surprised Dr Perinoff and hurried out of the field hospital. He typed a secure message about this discovery to Mission Commander Cussler on his wrist computer. A reply came back immediately: "Report to Mission HQ."

Commander Vision began to walk towards the mission commander's field office. He did not get far. Out of the corner of one of his genetically enhanced eyes, he caught a glimpse of something in the ultraviolet range. Vision looked in that direction as casually as he could, pretending to be interested in something else nearby. A blurry violet shape moved across the rubble. Commander Vision followed it. As he moved, he reported the sighting to Cussler via wrist computer. Then Vision alerted his team.

"Vision to Bug Team Alpha. Report to these coordinates," the commander said over the comm as he sent his location over his wrist computer.

"Yes, sir!" Lt Radar replied. "We're finishing some rescue work in Talos Shopping Centre. We're on our way."

Vision walked casually after the tall purple shape. It was roughly humanoid, just like what the team

had fought the night before. The figure did not seem to notice it was being followed. Commander Vision soon realized the figure was heading out of the city and towards the Talos Mine.

* * *

When the rest of the Bug Team caught up with the commander, he led them to the mining operation that had been a part of his life for many years. It was a place that had almost cost him that life.

"This place is incredible. It looks like a miniature city. Well, what's left of it," Spoor said as she looked at their surroundings. "Achooo! Sorry, sir. There's a lot of dirt in the air."

Spoor pinched her nasal flaps with her fingers.

"A miner would say, 'that's not dirt, that's wealth'," Vision replied as the team continued.

The Talos Mine was dug out of a 30-metre-high dome of rock sitting in the middle of the flat landscape. But that was only a small part of the mineral deposit. It was like an iceberg. Most of the valuable rock was spread out below the surface of the mine. Tunnels sloped deep down into the ground. The tunnels were reachable only by a single massive entry cut into the rock.

Several large ore preparation plants and numerous smelting and refining facilities surrounded the mine. All of the facilities were connected by overhead tracks that carried enormous buckets of raw ore out of the mine.

The buildings above ground were in ruins. Huge earthmovers, trucks the size of a small spacecraft, sat where the workers had left them when the evacuation order had been called.

"It looks like a ghost town," Radar observed.

"Complete with its own ghosts. Heads up!" Vision warned as he saw several purple figures step out from behind one of the big earthmovers and open fire.

Impact was bulky, but she was fast. She put herself between her teammates and the enemy barrage as soon as the first shots were fired. Her thick, beetle-DNA carapace deflected most of the blaster fire. That gave Locust time to leap in and use his carapace to block the rest of the enemy fire.

The rest of Bug Team Alpha returned fire at close range. One of the combatants was hit and turned visible to the human spectrum. A tall purple figure with multiple arms and legs appeared just as it began to flee.

"Hey! Can you all see that?" Burrow shouted.

"The blaster hit must have disrupted its conductive fluid and made it visible to the human eye," Vision realized.

"Its what?" Burrow asked.

"Just keep firing. I can see the rest of them. They're heading for the ore bins. Don't let them escape," Vision ordered.

CHAPTER 6

Commander Vision led Bug Team Alpha in pursuit of the enemy. He could see them clearly now, unlike the night before when the bright flashes of blaster fire interfered with his bug-enhanced vision.

"They're heading for the ore bins," the commander told his team. "Locust, make a bomb run. Head 'em off."

As soon as he gave the order, Vision could practically hear his father's voice yelling at him: "Don't compromise the mining equipment!" But then he recalled his conversation with Mission Commander Cussler. Vision would not let his history with the mine interfere with the mission.

Locust buzzed into the air. He sighted through his blaster's UV scope with one hand and tossed grenades at the enemy with the other. A line of explosions erupted in front of the figures as they ran towards a massive container of ore.

The container looked like a giant cart on wheels. It was seven metres tall and sat on tracks that led to a nearby smelting facility. Or what was left of one. The explosions filled the air with clouds of dirt and debris. Commander Vision charged straight into the thick haze Locust had created. The rest of the Bug Team followed. Locust hovered in the air but could no longer see the enemy.

"My scenting is useless in here," Lt Spoor warned as she pulled down her oxygen mask to protect her sensitive nasal filaments from the thick dust.

"I can't sense anything. The debris is messing with any vibes I could be detecting," Radar said.

"At least now we're the ones who are invisible. Spread out," Vision whispered over the comm.

"The enemy has stopped firing," Impact noted. "Either the explosives destroyed them or they're waiting in ambush."

Suddenly, blaster fire erupted at them from the ore bin.

"Ambush it is," Impact concluded.

"They've climbed up into the ore bin," Vision realized. "Take cover!"

The Bug Team returned fire as they ran for shelter in the ruins of the nearby smelting facility. Locust was forced from the air by enemy fire and joined his teammates.

For the time being, both the Bug Team members and the enemy were protected from each other. Vision considered the apparent stalemate. He looked out at the ore bin the enemy was hiding in, and then at the overhead track that held several enormous buckets of raw ore. One bucket was stalled directly over the ore bin.

"I have an idea," Vision said.

"What's the plan, Commander Vision?" Burrow asked.

"Be ready to rush the ore bin and rope up into it on my order," Vision told his team. "Locust, do you see that tower next to the bin?"

"Yes, sir," Locust replied.

"The booth at the top controls the buckets along the conveyor track. Get up there," Vision ordered.

"I see where you're going with this," Locust grinned.

"The team will climb up onto the rim of the bin and keep the enemy pinned down with blaster fire. Then Locust will drop the ore on them," Vision revealed.

"I like this plan," Impact said.

"Move out," Vision ordered.

The Bug Team charged out from the protection of the ruins, firing a blistering barrage at the ore bin. Locust flew up towards the control booth.

"Go for ascent!" the commander ordered.

Grappling lines were tossed in unison. The ropes hooked onto the lip of the ore bin. The team started to climb.

"Standing by to release the ore load," Locust reported over the comm from the control booth.

The Bug Team climbed up to the rim of the ore bin and stood on the edge. They aimed their blasters at the centre of the container. Their UV scopes revealed the violet shapes of a dozen enemy combatants. Only one of them was visible to the normal human range of vision. It lay on top of the ore in the bin and appeared to be bleeding a glowing liquid.

"Looks like we injured one of them," Spoor said.

"Fire at will," Vision ordered. "Locust, release your load."

Blaster fire blazed. The overhead conveyor bucket shuddered and froze. It did not drop its ore.

"The controls must be damaged," Vision realized. "Locust, you're going to have to operate the ore bucket manually."

"I'm on it," Locust replied.

Locust flew to the bucket and struggled with the heavy-duty release mechanism. It was crusted with rock dust and almost cemented in place. Enemy fire streaked at him from below. With one last massive tug, the mechanism clicked and the bucket tipped. Ore began raining down on the enemy below.

Suddenly, an explosion ripped through the entire structure. The control tower started to topple. It took the conveyor with it straight for Bug Team Alpha. Locust flew to safety. The Bug Team was on the perimeter of the bin and used their ropes to leap clear. The enemy was pinned in the centre of the bin. There was nowhere for them to go as the tower, the conveyor and the bucket full of ore crashed down on them.

Commander Vision hit the ground and rolled. He came to a stop just in time to see a single violet figure fleeing from the destruction. It ran into the main entrance of the mine, a few hundred metres away. Vision realized that this single being – whatever it was – must have somehow blown up the tower. It destroyed its own teammates in order to try to take out the Bug Team. He wondered if it was an act of sacrifice, or one of ruthlessness.

Bug Team Alpha converged around their commander.

"Well, your plan worked, sir. Sort of," Burrow said.

"Let's dig the bodies out from under that ore," Vision replied. "I'm hoping their invisibility got cancelled out once they died. I want a good look at them."

The Bug Team climbed back up into the ore bin. Burrow, Locust and Impact combined their strength to roll the ore bucket off the top of the bin, and then they started to clear away the rock that had been dumped on the combatants.

The team had to work around the twisted metal of the fallen control tower, but they soon cleared away the upper layers of ore. Finally, they encountered several large shards of a purple crystal. As the team carefully picked through the rocks, they discovered that most of the purple shards were covered with a glowing liquid.

"Crystalline blood," Vision said as he held several shards in his palm. "These shards are what's left of the enemy. Collect everything you can, team. I want to try to reassemble at least one of their bodies."

"That's some jigsaw puzzle, sir," Spoor remarked.

As the Bug Team sifted through the ore and host rocks, Vision noticed large chunks of an odd, iridescent crystal. The stones had an interior display of colour similar to opal, but Vision knew enough about mining gems to know that this was not opal. He knocked two chunks together to test their hardness. They didn't chip or break. They did not fracture or crack. They were not like anything he'd ever seen before, especially from the Talos Mine. The miners must have made a new discovery.

"Commander, we're finished, sir," Radar said.

Vision walked over to where the Bug Team had been piecing the purple shards together. They had cleared a patch of ground and had assembled a rough estimate of the invisible enemy's body. It was a tall, humanoid form with multiple arms and legs, a torso and head, all made of faceted crystal.

"We've been fighting rocks," Impact snorted in disgust.

"Rocks that bleed. Rocks that are probably alive," Vision corrected.

The commander looked over to where the enemy survivor had run into the mine entrance.

"There could be an army of them in there," Vision said. "I'm calling for reinforcements."

CHAPTER 7

Mission Commander Cussler diverted a company of troopers from evacuation efforts and sent them as backup for Bug Team Alpha. Cussler arrived at the mining operation along with Task Force Commander Kurosawa and 200 troopers. Commander Vision gave the two officers a more detailed brief of Bug Team's encounter with the enemy.

"We had them pinned down in an ore bin, but I believe that one of them blew the base of the control tower, destroying the others in the bin. It nearly got us too," Vision reported. "It escaped into the mine. However, I suspect that there are more of them down there. The tunnels and old shafts are perfect hiding places. There are sections of the mine that haven't been worked in decades."

"I'm going to need a map of the mine from Governor Boone," Cussler said to Commander Kurosawa.

"Yes, sir," Kurosawa replied and typed a message on his wrist computer.

"Sir, we know what they look like now," Vision told Cussler. "The Bug Team recovered what we could of the bodies and, well, reassembled one."

"Show me," the mission commander said.

Vision led Cussler and Kurosawa to the spot near the wrecked ore bin. Bug Team Alpha stayed with the remains, guarding them. They had covered the remains with an old, dusty tarp. Vision pulled back the covering. Cussler studied the broken crystalline body and shook his head.

"That's the weirdest thing I've ever seen, and I've seen a lot," Cussler commented.

"I still can't figure out what makes them invisible when they're alive, but they obviously turn visible when they're dead," Vision said.

"Commander Kurosawa, scan an image of the body and transmit it to your troops. I want them to know exactly what this 'invisible' enemy they're fighting looks like, even if it's just in its dead form," Cussler instructed.

Kurosawa had just completed his task when the map of the mine arrived. The schematic showed dozens of branching tunnels that went down dozens of levels.

"I see what you mean about being able to hide down there. It's a maze," Cussler observed.

The three officers studied the map. They conferred about where to search for the enemy and how to deploy their troops.

Suddenly, a loud string of furious language approached them. Vision recognized the voice. Cussler and Kurosawa looked up to see Governor Boone stomping towards them with his arms waving wildly.

"Kurosawa, deploy your men and start a grid search of the mine. It looks like I've got a skirmish coming in on another front. Dismissed," Cussler said as the governor approached.

Commander Vision was not dismissed, so he stood his ground in the face of the onslaught he knew was coming.

"That ore processing equipment was intact before the evacuation order! Now it's destroyed! Who authorized that? Who's responsible?" Governor Boone shouted as he pointed at the smashed control tower and ore conveyor.

"I consider the equipment an acceptable loss in the battle against the enemy," Cussler replied. "You should be grateful that only metal and machinery were destroyed instead of your son. He's discovered more about the enemy than anyone."

Governor Boone ignored the praise Cussler had for Commander Vision. The governor spun on his heel to face his son.

"You did this?" the governor gasped. "How many times have I said to never compromise the equipment? Never compromise the mining operation!"

Vision did not reply as his father yelled at him. Bug Team Alpha stood nearby and listened with growing discomfort. Locust buzzed his wings irritably. Radar flattened her antennae against her forehead. Cussler frowned and stepped between father and son.

"That's enough!" the mission commander barked. "You might be the colonial governor, Mr Boone, but that doesn't give you the authority to criticize my officer."

"Valuable property has been destroyed!" the governor insisted.

"Almost all of it was already destroyed by the enemy we're here to fight," Cussler responded. "A tower and a couple buckets of ore are hardly a major loss in the bigger picture."

"It's a major loss if we can't mine our new find," Governor Boone snapped. "Without that equipment we can't work the new deposit."

Commander Vision picked up one of the iridescent crystals he had found scattered in with the ore.

"Do you mean this?" Vision asked.

"What is it?" Cussler asked as he took the stone from his commander.

"We're not sure," the governor confessed. "The analysis so far points to it being a form of crystal that conducts energy more efficiently than anything ever discovered on any Coalition world. Its worth is incalculable."

"Super conductivity. Like the crystalline blood," Vision muttered. He held out his wrist computer towards the governor. "Show me the schematics of the deposit."

"No! It's private company information," Governor Boone said.

"Are you refusing to cooperate with a sanctioned military mission?" Cussler asked coldly.

"Uh, no," the governor replied.

"Then transmit the location to my officer," Cussler instructed.

As the governor grudgingly transferred the information to Vision's wrist computer, the mine entrance suddenly spewed dirt and debris.

"That's a windblast! There's been a collapse!" Vision said.

Cussler, Vision and the Bug Team sprinted towards the mine entrance a few hundred metres away. The command comm erupted with confused chatter. Blaster fire echoed up out of the main tunnel.

"We're under attack!" Kurosawa's voice shouted over the comm.

"Bug Team Alpha! Go! Go! Go!" Cussler ordered.

Commander Vision led his team into the mine and down the wide main artery tunnel. For Vision it was like going back in time. He had been down this route every day when he was a kid. But nothing like this had ever happened at the Talos Mine – until his accident.

The Bug Team Alpha members put on their helmets and oxygen masks and switched on the helmet lights as they worked their way through the thick, choking cloud of dirt and debris.

Lt Radar's antennae swept for vibrations. All the tiny particles in the air interfered with her attempt at detection. It was like trying to see through a thick fog. Suddenly, she picked up a large mass heading towards the Bug Team.

"Something's coming our way! I . . . I'm not quite sure what it could be, sir!" Radar reported over the comm.

A large group of wounded soldiers from Kurosawa's company staggered through the haze. They were covered with glowing crystalline blood. The troops had obviously engaged the enemy.

"Vision to Cussler! We need medical teams!" the commander reported over the comm.

"They're on their way," Cussler replied crisply. He had deployed them as soon as the windblast had happened.

As the Bug Team pressed deeper down the tunnel, they met more troops in retreat. At last they arrived at the point of encounter.

The dust was settling here. Injured soldiers lay sprawled among fallen crystalline combatants. A few soldiers, splattered with crystalline blood, helped each other hobble out of the area.

"I'm getting vibes of a collapse up ahead," Radar reported.

The Bug Team found a wall of rubble blocking the tunnel. Soldiers were half buried in the fallen rocks. Among those soldiers were Private Margate and his buddies.

"You guys just can't stay out of trouble," Burrow sighed as he used his spikes to dig them out.

CHAPTER 8

At first Private Margate and his pals seemed as if they were going to refuse help from "those altered guys." But their attitude changed as Burrow, Impact and Locust made short work of removing the heavy stones. Radar and Spoor pitched in. Commander Vision offered his hand to Margate to help the trooper out of the rubble.

"Thanks, sir," Margate mumbled.

"Where's Commander Kurosawa?" Vision asked. "I can't raise him on the comm."

"He was further down the tunnel when the enemy attacked and the roof collapsed," Margate reported.

"I'm picking up blaster fire from the other side of the rock fall," Radar announced as she pressed her cranial antennae against the surface of the fallen rocks.

"We've got to get to them," Vision said. "This blockage is too big even for Burrow to get through in time. Explosives are too risky. We need a heavy-duty earthmover. And I know just where to get one."

Commander Vision sprinted back down the tunnel and out of the mine. Several ore trucks and earthmovers sat near the wrecked conveyor. Vision climbed up into one of the giant vehicles and revved it to life. A moment later the earthmover was bouncing down the tunnel on its humongous tyres at top speed. The personnel still in the tunnel heard the machine coming and flattened against the walls. The Bug Team cleared the area around the rock fall just before Commander Vision rammed the earthmover into it.

Beep! Beep! Beep! The earthmover backed up. Its massive front scoop was full of rubble. Suddenly, the rest of the rocks came apart and formed an opening.

"There's still a firefight on the other side!" Radar shouted, even though everyone could hear the blasts.

Vision drove the massive earthmover forwards again and smashed through the hole. The rock fall fell apart. The Bug Team followed him through the breach. Private Margate and his pals followed the Bug Team.

They found Commander Kurosawa and several squads of soldiers battling the enemy. The attackers were vaguely visible in the light of the UV scopes, but Vision had no problem seeing them clearly.

"Troops! Stand back!" Vision yelled to the soldiers as he used the earthmover to ram a large group of the crystalline combatants. They shattered like glass. Kurosawa's troops surged forwards again to engage the rest. Vision paused the vehicle only long enough to motion his team to climb aboard. Once all were on, he accelerated the giant machine further down the tunnel.

"Where are we going, sir?" Spoor asked over her comm. It looked as if Vision was abandoning the fight.

"I want to investigate the section of the mine where the iridescent crystals were found," the commander replied. "I want to examine the deposit firsthand. My father said that the crystal was super-conductive. So is the crystalline blood. I think there's a connection."

Unexpectedly, the enemy broke off their attack on the troops and turned to chase the earthmover. Kurosawa ordered an immediate pursuit of the enemy. Blaster fire streaked around the earthmover, but the vehicle soon outpaced the enemy. Vision followed the map on his wrist computer to the new deposit. It took him into a section of the Talos Mine he had never seen before. He brought the earthmover to a halt. They had reached a T-junction that was too small for the massive vehicle. The Bug Team climbed down from the machine and Vision double-checked his wrist computer.

"Both these tunnels are marked in red on the map," the commander said. "That means it's restricted. But why? I thought they were working this deposit."

"I'm getting vibes down the left-hand tunnel," Radar said. "High-register frequencies. Huh. It stopped."

"Let's go," Vision said. The Bug Team quickly reached a deep shaft at the end of the tunnel. Their helmet lights illuminated a large, vertical vein of iridescent crystal that followed the shaft down into the darkness.

"That's the same stuff from the ore bin," Spoor observed.

A rumbling sound came up from below. The Bug Team tensed.

"Here's our ride," Vision explained. He stood next to a roughly wired control box mounted on the rock wall. A crude platform rose up out of the shaft.

"What's this thing made from? Toothpicks and string?" Impact said as they stepped onto the platform.

"It might not look like much, but it'll hold several hundred kilograms of ore," Vision assured them.

The lift reached the bottom of the shaft. The Bug Team stepped into a tunnel carved out of solid iridescent crystal. As soon as their boots made contact with the material, Radar's antennae jerked wildly. She clapped her hands to her forehead and bent over in pain.

"Ahhhh! I'm getting hit by high-frequency sonic blasts," Radar groaned.

Suddenly, Commander Vision reacted in a similar manner. He shielded his eyes with his hands and doubled over. "Gaaagh! There's some kind of high-intensity light!" he gasped.

"Huh? I don't see or hear anything," Locust said.

"Neither do we," the rest of the team agreed.

"It's ultraviolet light," Vision realized. "It's coming from the crystal!"

Commander Vision staggered. He put his hand on the tunnel wall to keep himself from falling. As he touched the crystal, the light and sound onslaught stopped.

"I never thought that this material might have sonic or radiant properties," Vision said as he and Radar tried to recover.

"Maybe you and Radar are the only ones who can see or hear it," Spoor suggested.

"Uh, can anyone else see that?" Burrow asked as he pointed at one of the walls.

A portion of the wall was turning from a solid crystal into a thick, gooey liquid. The substance dripped down to the floor and started to pool near their feet. The Bug Team backed away from it instinctively. Except for Commander Vision. He stepped towards the liquid and concentrated his light on it. He studied it with his DNA-enhanced sight. Curious, he reached out and touched the glowing liquid with his gloved hand and lifted it up to get a better look at the substance.

"It's the same stuff as the crystalline blood from the enemy," the commander announced.

Suddenly, the liquid on his glove turned into small shards of purple crystal. The shards started to grow up the commander's arm like frost across a window. The liquid on the ground started to transform into purple crystalline combatants. The enemy was growing in front of their eyes.

CHAPTER 9

The Bug Team now faced danger on two fronts. Enemy combatants were rising up out of the pool of crystalline blood as the purple crystals accelerated up Commander Vision's arm. The team took aim at the enemy while Impact balled her fists and used them like sledgehammers to smash the purple crystals crawling up the commander's arm. Slivers flew in every direction. One of them cut into the commander's cheek, drawing blood. He instinctively wiped it away with his glove – the one with the crystalline blood still on it.

When Vision's blood met the crystalline blood, the commander felt a burst of pain in his head. Then it began to pulse like a heartbeat. Between the beats images flashed through his mind. He saw what looked like lightning travelling along crystalline pathways the way electrical impulses ran along nerves. Sparks jumped between clusters of these pathways as if between synapses in a brain. There were clusters of these clusters in an ever-expanding sphere. At last the commander saw dozens of these spheres connected by hundreds of crystalline pathways. Suddenly, he knew what it was. He knew *where* he was.

"I'm inside the mind of a living being," Vision thought. "I'm inside the brain of a crystalline entity."

The commander heard the voices of his team as if they were far away. They were shouting to him in alarm. Vision turned his attention to the voices, and suddenly he came back to reality. He saw the Bug Team with their weapons drawn, ready for action. They stood between him and a line of purple enemy combatants. The crystalline soldiers stood in the pool of liquid from which they had grown. They did not move or make any attempt to attack the Bug Team.

"Stand down!" Vision ordered the team. "I think I know what's going on."

"Commander! Are you all right? You just . . . stopped moving," Spoor said.

"Believe it or not, I was talking to them," Vision said. "Well, one of them, anyway. I was inside its head."

"What?" Locust blurted. He did not take his eyes off the enemy standing in front of him.

"These crystals are alive, and they want to communicate with us," the commander said. He stripped off his combat gloves. "We have to make physical contact. Take off your gloves and link hands."

The command was an odd one, but Bug Team Alpha obeyed. They watched the crystalline enemy warily, ready for any move. They slung back their weapons, took off their combat gloves, and held hands with Vision. Then the commander reached out to the nearest crystalline combatant.

The crystalline creatures also all joined their hands together. The one nearest to Vision grasped his hand.

"We have to complete the circuit," Vision said. "Radar, you're the missing link. Please take the purple guy's hand."

"Yes, sir," Radar said reluctantly. She reached out and grasped the creature's hand to form a circle.

Bug Team members immediately saw images of a vast network of crystal veins running under the capital city of Talos and all through the surrounding area. The veins were all connected to a single sphere of crystal under the Talos Mine, like blood vessels to a heart.

"We're talking to the crystal sphere under the Talos Mine," Vision thought. His team heard him inside their heads.

Another wave of communication hit the Bug Team. This time they felt the vibrations of the mining operation digging close to the crystalline veins and nerves. They felt the pain of those nerves being gouged and dug out. Then came the agony of the central sphere, the brain itself, being drilled into and removed bit by bit.

Then the Bug Team saw liquid crystalline blood seep out of the central sphere. Purple crystals formed and grew. The enemy combatants! They watched the crystalline beings rise up from the iridescent veins under Talos and attack the city with energy blasts. But the blasts did not come from weapons. The energy was generated by and channelled through the super-conductive fluid in their crystalline bodies. It was discharged through their hands. They were living weapons! The combatants were like antibodies. They were created as a natural response to an attack on the living "body" of the entity. The tunnel the team was standing in was actually a severe injury caused by the Talos miners.

"I'm going to fix this," Vision thought with conviction. "I don't know how, but I will find a way."

A wave of relief from the entity washed over the Bug Team.

"Truce?" Vision asked the entity. He received an image of the crystalline combatants turning to liquid and being absorbed back into the iridescent veins.

Bug Team Alpha released their hands. The purple enemy soldiers disappeared. So did the pool of liquid that had created them.

"They've been reabsorbed. I think we have a truce," Vision concluded. "Let's get back to the surface and uphold our end of the bargain."

The commander led his team back to the lift. As they stepped onto the platform and began to ascend, Vision tried to contact Mission Commander Cussler. He wanted to let Cussler know about the truce.

"I can't get a signal," Vision said. "Either we're too deep in the mine or the crystalline vein is interfering with transmission. Or both."

Suddenly, they heard the sound of a tremendous boom. The lift platform shook violently and so did the shaft it was in. Dirt and pieces of rock sheared off the walls and fell on the Bug Team. The platform shuddered and lurched to a halt halfway up the shaft.

"Locust, go topside and see what happened," Vision said.

Locust had just enough room in the shaft to deploy his wings and buzz upwards. He returned moments later.

"The good news is that the tunnel above is intact all the way back to the earthmover. The bad news is that most of the earthmover is buried under a huge rock fall," Locust said.

"Not for long," Burrow declared and flexed his spiked arms.

"We've got to get up there first," Spoor pointed out.

The team looked up at the long, dark shaft.

"I can take you one by one," Locust volunteered.

"Start with Radar," Vision said. "She can start to scan the rock fall and locate any weak points."

"Race ya!" Burrow said and started to spike his way up the side of the shaft.

Locust wrapped his arms around Radar and launched upwards.

CHAPTER 10

The Bug Team Alpha members convened at the earthmover. Commander Vision assessed the rock fall with a miner's eye.

"This rock is highly compacted. It's going to be tough to get through," Vision said.

"I did a scan of the rock fall, sir. I could not detect any significant weak points or voids, either," Radar reported.

"There aren't any scents or odours coming through. That means no air gaps in the collapsed material," Spoor added.

"I'm up for the challenge," Burrow declared. He flexed his bug arms and started to dig through the rock, quickly throwing piece after piece into a pile behind him.

He dug. And dug. And dug. Even with the help of Impact's strength and the rest of the team, Burrow could not seem to reach the other side.

"There's no way to know how far back the collapse goes," Radar said as she leaned tiredly against the machine's huge scoop. "I can't sense where it ends."

"No wonder there's no air coming through," Spoor concluded.

"Are we going to run out of oxygen?" Locust asked, suddenly alarmed. "Are we buried alive?"

"Those rock people did this. They blew up the tunnel to trap us down here. Some truce!" Impact growled.

"Stop the chatter, Bug Team! Stay focused," Commander Vision barked. He gestured at the second tunnel branching off from the T-junction. "We'll follow this tunnel. The map shows it's a dead end, but let's see for ourselves."

The Bug Team walked down the passage until they reached a vertical vein of iridescent crystal running from floor to ceiling where miners had drilled exploratory boreholes into the vein. But there was no way out that the team members could see.

"What are we going to do, sir?" Locust asked nervously.

"Maybe I can communicate with the entity again," Vision replied. "These rock strata are its home. Maybe it can show me a way out."

Vision took off one of his combat gloves and placed his bare hand on the vein of iridescent crystal.

"We need to get to the surface," Vision whispered. The crystal glowed in response.

"Whoa! I'm getting seriously strong vibes!" Radar announced.

Suddenly, the vein started to shudder under Vision's hand. The vibration got stronger and stronger until the host rock around the vein began to crumble. The Bug Team jumped back as rubble fell away to form a slim shaft.

When the shaking stopped, there was a vertical passageway that followed the crystal vein upwards. Vision climbed over the pile of rubble and peered up the shaft.

"I can see daylight!" he exclaimed. He patted the vein of crystal gently. "Thank you."

The commander deployed Burrow first, who used his strong bug arms and legs to climb up the host rock in the shaft. Burrow gouged out handholds into the rock for his teammates. He was careful not to hit the crystal vein.

Impact followed and used her powerful fists to punch the handholds and expand them. Locust came after her. He deployed his thick wing carapace to act like an umbrella to shield the rest of the team below from the falling debris created by Burrow and Impact.

Radar and Spoor followed Locust. Commander Vision brought up the rear.

Bug Team Alpha soon emerged amid the ruins of a collapsed building.

"Where in Talos are we?" Spoor wondered as she stood on top of the rubble and looked around.

"It's where we wounded the enemy last night," Vision said.

The Bug Team commander pointed to the traces of crystalline blood still on the broken masonry.

"Now we know how they disappeared," Vision continued. "They went underground. Or, more accurately, they were probably reabsorbed by the crystal vein we just followed up here."

"Well, we're on the surface. The crystalline entity kept its end of the bargain. How do we keep ours?" Spoor said.

"I have an idea," Vision replied. "The entity is wounded, so I can pack and seal the wound. I think that will allow it to heal. But I'm going to need a lot of polycrete."

Commander Vision immediately contacted Mission Commander Cussler to report his location and tell him about his plan.

"We thought you were trapped or killed in that cave-in," Cussler said.

"We would have been if not for the crystalline entity helping us," Vision replied. "But we've called a truce and . . ."

"Wait. The crystalline what?" Cussler asked.

"There's an intelligent being down there made of crystal. The veins that are being mined are literally its veins," Vision said. "The invisible combatants we've been fighting are its antibodies. They exist in the ultraviolet spectrum that humans can't see."

"Wait a minute, Vision. Let me get this straight. The attacker is an intelligent entity that lives in the mine. It attacked because it's been injured from the mining, and you promised to heal it?" Cussler asked.

"Yes, sir. I communicated with it," Vision replied. "It's injured. I promised to help. But I need polycrete. The Coalition ships brought plenty of it to construct temporary field offices and medical buildings. Request permission to get what I need from one of the supply depots."

"Very well. I'm transmitting the requisition code right now," Cussler said.

A short time later, Bug Team Alpha drove back to the Talos Mine in a supply vehicle loaded with bags of dry polycrete. Locust flew overhead and sang an old cavalry song. Impact and Burrow sat on top of the bags of polycrete in the back of the truck while Radar and Spoor rode in the cab with their commander.

When they arrived at the mine, Commander Vision drove past the medical field hospital that had sprung up to treat the injured troopers. Mission

Commander Cussler stood in front of the entrance and waved the Bug Team through.

Commander Vision continued driving the truck down the main tunnel. There was no sign of the crystalline combatants. The truce was holding.

When the Bug Team reached the cave-in that had buried the earthmover, they found Kurosawa and his troopers trying to dig it out.

"Commander Vision! Commander Cussler just informed me about your plan to heal a . . . the rock being?" Kurosawa asked.

"Yes, but we've got to get past that cave-in, first," Vision replied.

"Hey! You guys are alive! We thought you were under all that rock!" Private Margate exclaimed when he saw the Bug Team. "Wait a second. How did you guys get out?"

"Long story. Trouble is, now we have to get back in," Impact replied.

Suddenly, the whole tunnel started to shake. The Coalition troops retreated from the rock fall as it started to break apart. A large opening appeared.

"The entity knows we're here," Vision concluded. "It's clearing the way."

"I knew it had blocked the way in the first place," Impact said. "But it was probably only trying to protect itself."

"We'll take it from here, commander," Vision told Kurosawa.

Commander Vision drove the small supply truck through the opening and down the tunnel to the lift platform. He discovered that it was only a loose wire that had stopped it earlier. He quickly fixed it and raised the platform the remainder of the way.

The team loaded the bags of polycrete onto the platform and descended into the crystalline tunnel. They quickly spread dry polycrete on the floor of the tunnel, as far back as the excavation went. Vision dispersed a small packet of activator granules and the polycrete foamed, expanded and filled the iridescent tunnel.

A few minutes later, the polycrete was solid as rock.

"Packed and sealed. Mission accomplished," Vision said.

Commander Vision then placed his hand on the exterior of the sealed tunnel and whispered, "Get well and be safe."

Bug Team Alpha drove back through the main mine tunnels, which were now empty of all troops and crystalline combatants. They emerged from the mine and climbed out of the vehicle.

Private Margate and his pals were waiting for them. The Bug Team members were surprised when the troopers shook their hands and pounded them on their armour like comrades.

"You saved our lives in there," Margate said. "You guys are all right."

The troopers left when they saw Governor Boone approach. Vision faced his father, eye to eye. He was ready for anything his father might say, except for his father's praise.

"The attacks have stopped. You saved the mine. You saved Talos," the governor said. "You did good, son."

"Uh, thank you, sir," Vision replied in surprise.

"I wish you'd stayed in Talos, but you're good at what you do now," his father admitted. "Commander of an elite team and all that."

"They're the best in the Colonial Armed Forces," Vision stated proudly.

"Why don't you tell me all about them . . . over dinner," Governor Boone suggested. He put his hand on his son's shoulder lightly.

"I'd like that . . . Dad," Vision replied with a small smile.

Bug Team Alpha stood nearby and watched the reunion unfold.

"It looks like the crystalline entity isn't the only thing that got healed today," Spoor whispered to her teammates.

Mission report

TO: GENERAL JAMES CLAUDIUS BARRETT,
COMMANDER OF COLONIAL ARMED FORCES

FROM: COMMANDER JACKSON "VISION" BOONE,
BUG TEAM ALPHA

SUBJECT: AFTER ACTION REPORT

MISSION DETAILS:

Mission Planet: Hephaestus
Mission Parameters: Defend and protect;
  search and rescue
Mission Team: Bug Team Alpha [BTA]
* Commander Jackson "Vision" Boone
* Lt Anushka "Spoor" Kumar
* Lt Akiko "Radar" Murasaki
* Lt Irene "Impact" Mallory
* Lt Gustav "Burrow" Von Braun
* Lt Sancho "Locust" Castillo

MISSION SUMMARY:

Bug Team Alpha was dispatched to Talos, capital city of Earth Colonial Coalition planet Hephaestus, in response to reports of attacks by invisible, unknown hostiles. BTA assignment was part of larger Colonial Armed Forces mission under the direction of Mission Commander Preston Cussler. BTA attached to task force unit under command of Commander Wajima Kurosawa.

Upon arrival, 50 per cent of city was observed destroyed. Defend and protect designation was then changed to search and rescue. Surviving citizens were discovered in decimated city. BTA participated in search and rescue operations. Live recovery of citizens and Colonial Governor Jefferson Boone accomplished.

During recovery operations, BTA engaged the combatant within the city limits. BTA obtained a sample of enemy life form. Analysis revealed that the enemy was a crystalline life form. A second encounter with the enemy occurred at the Talos Mine. BTA located enemy point of origin inside the mine. Coalition Armed Forces later engaged the enemy inside the Talos Mine.

BTA made contact with the invisible enemy. BTA discovered the crystalline enemy life forms were defensive "antibodies" protecting a crystalline intelligence living within the Talos Mine. Mining excavations had wounded the crystalline intelligence. The attacks on Talos and its inhabitants were acts of self-defence.

BTA was authorized to use quantities of polycrete to fill and seal the excavation site, allowing the wound to heal. BTA accomplished this goal.

This portion of the Talos Mine has been shut down permanently.

APPENDIX 1: EQUIPMENT REQUISITION
Heavy Payload Transport Truck: 1
Bags Dry Polycrete [with activator packs]: 50

APPENDIX 2: PARTICIPANTS:
Mission Commander Preston Cussler
Task Force Commander Wajima Kurosawa
Bug Team Alpha [mission participants listed above]
Colonial Governor Jefferson Boone

END REPORT

Glossary

combatant someone or something that is engaged or ready to engage in combat

crystalline having a crystal-like quality

DNA molecule that carries all of the instructions to make a living thing and keep it working; DNA is short for deoxyribonucleic acid

entity something that exists as a single or independent unit

genetic relating to physical traits or conditions passed down from parents to children

iridescent having colours that seem to change at different angles

polycrete very strong cement used in buildings

ultraviolet rays of light that cannot be seen by the human eye

About the author

Laurie S Sutton has been interested in science fiction ever since she first saw the *Sputnik* satellite speed across the night sky as a very young child. By 12 years old, she was reading books by classic sci-fi authors Robert Heinlein, Isaac Azimov and Arthur C Clarke. Then she discovered *STAR TREK*.

Laurie's love of outer space has led her to write *STAR TREK* comics for *DC* Comics, *Malibu* Comics and *Marvel* Comics. From her home in Florida, USA, she has watched many Space Shuttle launches blaze a trail though the sky. Now she watches the night sky as the International Space Station sails overhead instead of *Sputnik*.

About the illustrator

James Nathaniel is a digital comic book artist and illustrator from the UK. With a graphics tablet and pen, he produces dramatic narrative focused fantasy, science fiction and non-fiction work. His work is the result of inspiration accumulated from the likes of Sean Gordon Murphy, Jake Wyatt, Jamie Hewlett and Jon Foster, as well many years playing video games and watching films. In the near future, James hopes to write and illustrate his own graphic novels from stories he's been developing over the years.

Discussion questions

1. The people of Talos have been mining on the planet Hephaestus for a very long time. Then a new discovery in the mine revolts against the people. Do you think the crystalline entity was justified in the way it revolted against the people of Talos? Explain why or why not?

2. Some of the troops Bug Team Alpha encounters at the beginning of the mission are rude to them. Private Margate is cut off from using the word "freak" to describe them. Vision's choice to join Bug Team Alpha hurt his relationship with his father. Do you think these reactions to Bug Team Alpha are appropriate? Explain why or why not?

3. What makes an invisible enemy more difficult than one you can see? Is there any advantage to fighting an enemy you can't see? Explain your answer.

1. Imagine you were a member of Bug Team Alpha. What bug or insect would you model your new body after? Using descriptive language, write about what physical features and elite fighting skills you would have.

2. Commander Vision must assure Commander Cussler that his past in Talos won't affect his ability to complete the mission. Was there ever a time you left a place and were uncomfortable when you had to go back? Or a time you had to forget about your past in order to move on? Write about the situation and how you handled it.

3. What happens next in the story? You decide! Does sealing the mine work to keep the crystalline entity at bay? Does Commander Vision stay in Talos and spend time with his father? What is their new relationship like? What do the other members of Bug Team Alpha do next?

BUG TEAM ALPHA

BUG TEAM ALPHA

THE DIG

When an archaeologist goes missing and presumed kidnapped during an expedition, Bug Team Alpha is called in to help.

BUG TEAM ALPHA

THE DRACO

The president of Earth has been kidnapped by Draco warrior forces. Can Bug Team Alpha rescue her in time?

BUG TEAM ALPHA

INVISIBLE ENEMY

Talos is under attack, but no one can see exactly who - or what - the enemy is. Bug Team Alpha is called in to fight.

BUG TEAM ALPHA

STRANDED

What happens when Bug Team Alpha's transport ship crash lands after intersecting an interplanetary war zone? Read *Stranded* to find out!